The Radical Undersea Journey of Mr. Dude

Special thanks to Joel Harper for the good vibes, guidance and helping make this book happen and Wing Lam for the inspiration.

Published by Vote The Ocean.

For more information, visit VoteTheOcean.org

I dedicate this book to my beautiful son, Vipe, and his wrecking crew:
Billie, Charlotte, Dani, Demi, Emma, Fiona, Gunny, Ivana, Jack, Jason, Jayden, Lillian, Mia, Naz, Rylee, Sadie, Scarlett, Stella, Tanner, and Tucker.

Protect what you love.

When the sun hit his eyes, and the smell of surf filled his nose, it was time for Mr. Dude to jump out of bed and grab his surfboard.

Before heading out to sea, he had to fuel up!

Mr. Dude grabbed some orange juice from a plastic cup.

Slurp!

He gulped it down with a plastic straw. He loved plastic straws because they were so fun to drink from.

Mr. Dude tossed his plastic cup and plastic straw into the garbage.

Burrrrrp!

He grabbed his board. It was time to hit the waves!

On the beach, in the sun and surf,
Mr. Dude took a deep breath.

He smiled and paddled out on the rolling sea, ready to catch the perfect wave!

A huge wave rolled in, so Mr. Dude got ready.

But, then, something caught his eye.

There was an old, black tire floating in the water, and Mr. Dude was headed straight for it. Mr. Dude's surfboard hit the tire and he flew straight into the air.

Suddenly Mr. Dude was underwater,
tumbling up and down
and round and round like
he was in a washing machine.

Strangely, he saw his reflection on the surface of a shiny stone.

Mr. Dude had turned into a fish!

How could that be? It's impossible, he thought.

It was true, though.

Mr. Dude had turned into a Dude fish!

He saw so many colorful creatures underwater, the sun shinning on them from above.

There were big green turtles, blue and yellow fish and bright red starfish.

There were lobsters too, reddish-brown in color.

And there was a sea lion with a big mustache who waved at the Dude fish.

"Hey, Dude," said the sea lion.

"Where am I?" asked Mr. Dude.

The big green turtle swam over and said, "You're in the Pacific Ocean, of course. We all live here, but I've never seen a fish like you before. Where are you from?"

Mr. Dude said "I'm a human. I mean, I don't look like it, but I'm a surfer from up above. I live on land but surf the waves and something happened that made me into a fish."

"How'd you get down here?" asked the lobster.

"I don't know," said Mr. Dude, rubbing his head. "Oh wait, I remember now. My surfboard hit a tire."

"There are all kinds of strange and ugly things down here," the turtle said. "Come with us and we'll show you."

The turtle and the sea lion swam ahead. Mr. Dude followed them. Soon more fish and underwater creatures joined them.

"See?" said the turtle. He pointed a fin at a strange pile of weird shapes.

"Look at this, Mr. Dude. It's plastic."

Mr. Dude swam over, shook his head and said. "I can't believe it, man. Look at all this garbage! I mean, here are plastic straws...and soda bottles...and plastic bags. We humans are throwing all this in the ocean?"

"That's right, dude." the lobster said. "And it collects in the water, trapping fish, lobsters, and all kinds of animals. It makes the water gross and unhealthy for us."

Soon, a sun fish swam by.

"I think we should take Mr. Dude to meet Hugh," said the sun fish.

All the fish and creatures suddenly became quiet. What little sunshine came through the gross plastic twinkled on their scales and fins.

"Uh, man, who's Hugh?" asked Mr. Dude.

"You'll see," said the turtle. "Let's go!"

The sun fish led the way, swimming past schools of fish and around a coral reef until they reached a big, dark cave.

"Hugh," said the sun fish. "We brought you someone. He's a human. His name is Mr. Dude and he's a nice surfer from up top."

Hugh the shark said, "We need help from your kind, Mr. Dude. Did you see all the plastic? All the garbage that humans have thrown into the ocean?"

"Oh my, Hugh, did I ever, said Mr. Dude. I'm so sorry big guy. I didn't know and I'm never going to use plastic again!"

"Be responsible, Mr. Dude," said Hugh. "Go back up top, teach people to refuse, reduce, reuse and recycle, and tell them your story and what you've seen down here."

Mr. Dude said goodbye to Hugh the shark, the turtle, sun fish, lobster, and the sea lion.

It was time to get back up to the surface and go home.

When he reached the surface, the fins were gone! He wasn't a fish anymore, just a Dude again.

"Hey, Mr. Dude!" said another surfer. "That was quite the wipeout, man. You okay?"

Mr. Dude nodded, grabbing his surfboard and walking onto the beach.

"Yeah, man. I'm fine. Better than fine!"

He was excited and ready to change things.

From that day forward, Mr. Dude took the pledge to refuse, reduce, reuse, and recycle all his trash.

He took his message to the local school and told all the kids about the plastic he saw. They could hardly believe his adventure but his story was so convicing, they all pledged to...

Make a promise to uphold the KindHumans and Vote The Ocean junior environmental voter pledge. Take a picture with this page and post it to your social media page to share with your friends and family. Tag us at #VoteTheOcean so we can see your pledge.

I give my pledge to save and faithfully to defend from waste the natural resources of my country, its air, soil and minerals and its forests, waters and wildlife.

kindhumans
kindhumans.com

Vipe Desai, Author

Once the ocean embraces you, its all over. And that's exactly how it started for Vipe. It was an oceanography school field trip where he first set his eyes on the ocean and all its wonders that set Vipe on a lifelong journey of caring for the ocean. It continued with his love for surfing, launching Vote The Ocean and all the way to Washington D.C. to testify before members of Congress on why protecting our ocean is important for our coastal communities. Today, Vipe and his family enjoy spending every chance they get at the beach, whether its playing in the sand, snorkeling along the shoreline or catching waves - they are committed to protecting what they love.

Ashley Casalino, Illustrator

My name is Ashley Casalino. I am an artist that currently lives in a mountain town called, Colorado Springs, Co. Creating is what I wake up every morning for. I feel inspired by the trees on a walk with my children or even by the stories that they tell me. Follow my artistic journey on my Instagram: @ashley_casalino
www.ashleycasalino.com

Made in the USA
Monee, IL
24 December 2020